The Black Hole of Glenranald

E.W. Hornung

Table of Contents

The Black Hole of Glenranald

E.W. Hornung

IT was coming up the Murrumbidgee that Fergus Carrick first heard the name of Stingaree. With the cautious enterprise of his race, the young gentleman had booked steerage on a river steamer whose solitary passenger he proved to be; accordingly he was not only permitted to sleep on the saloon settee at nights, but graciously bidden to the captain's board by day. It was there that Fergus Carrick encouraged tales of the bushrangers as the one cleanly topic familiar in the mouth of the elderly engineer who completed the party. And it seemed that the knighthood of the up–country road had been an extinct order from the extirpation of the Kellys to the appearance of this same Stingaree, who was reported a man of birth and mystery, with an ostentatious passion for music and as romantic a method as that of any highwayman of the Old World from which he hailed. But the callow Fergus had been spared the romantic temperament, and was less impressed than entertained with what he heard.

On his arrival at Glenranald, however, he found that substantial township shaking with laughter over the outlaw's latest and least discreditable exploit, at the back–block hamlet of Yallarook; and then it was that young Carrick first conceived an ambition to open his Colonial career with the capture of Stingaree; for he was a serious immigrant, who had come out in his teens, to stay out, if necessary, for the term of his natural life.

The idea had birth under one of the many pine trees which shaded the skeleton streets of budding Glenranald. On this tree was nailed a placard offering high reward for the bushranger's person alive or dead. Fergus was making an immediate note in his pocketbook when a hand fell on his shoulder.

"Would ye like the half o' yon?" inquired a voice in his own tongue; and there at his elbow stood an elderly gentleman, whose patriarchal beard hid half the buttons of his alpaca coat, while a black skull–cap sat somewhat jauntily on his head.

"What do you mean?" said Fergus, bluntly, for the old gentleman stood chuckling gently in his venerable beard.

"To lay a hold of him," replied the other, "with the help o' some younger and abler–bodied man; and you're the very one I want."

The raw youth stared ingenuously.

"But what can you know about me?"

"I saw ye land at the wharf," said the old gentleman, nodding his approval of the question, "and says I, 'That's my man,' as soon as ever I clapped eyes on ye. So I had a crack wi' the captain o' yon steamer; he told me you hadna a billet, but were just on the lookout for the best ye could get, an' that's all he'd been able to get out o' ye in a five days' voyage. That was enough for me. I want a man who can keep his tongue behind his teeth, and I wanted you before I knew you were a brither Scot!"

"Are you a squatter, sir?" the young man asked, a little overwhelmed.

"No, sir, I'm branch manager o' the Bank o' New South Wales, the only bank within a hunder miles o' where we stand; and I can offer ye a better billet than any squatter in the Colony."

"Indeed? I'm sure you're very kind, sir, but I'm wanting to get on a station," protested Fergus with all his tact. "And as a matter of fact, I have introductions to one or two stations further back, though I saw no reason to tell our friend the skipper so."

"Quite right, quite right! I like a man who can keep his tongue in its kennel!" cried the bank manager, rubbing his hands. "But wait while I tell ye: ye'd need to work for your

2

rations an any station I ever heard tell of, and I keep the accounts of enough to know. Now, with me, ye'd get two pound a week till your share o' the reward was wiped off; and if we had no luck for a year you'd be no worse off, but could go and try your squatters then. That's a promise, and I'll keep it as sure as my name's Andr' Macbean!"

"But how do you propose to catch this fellow, Mr. Macbean?"

The bank manager looked on all sides, likewise behind the tree, before replying under his breath: "By setting a wee trap for him! A bank's a bank, and Stingaree hasna stuck one up since he took to his trade. But I'll tell ye no more till ye give me your answer. Yes or no?"

"I'm afraid I don't even write an office hand; and as for figures ——"

Mr. Macbean laughed outright.

"Did I say I was going to take ye into the bank, mun?" cried he. "There's three of us already to do the writin' an' the cipherin,' an' three's enough. Can you ride?"

"I have ridden."

"And ye'll do any rough job I set ye to?"

"The rougher the better."

"That's all I ask. There's a buggy and a pair for ye to mind, and mebbe drive, though it's horseback errands you'll do most of. I'm an old widower living alone with an aged housekeeper. The cashier and the clerk dig in the township, and I need to have a man of some sort about the place; in fact, I have one, but I'll soon get rid of him if you'll come instead. Understand, you live in the house with me, just like the jackeroos on the stations; and like the jackeroos, you do all the odd jobs and dirty work that no one else'll look at; but, unlike them, you get two pounds a week from the first for doing it."

Mr. Andrew Macbean had chanced upon a magic word. It was the position of "jackeroo," or utility parlor–man, on one or other of the stations to which he carried introductions, that his young countryman had set before him as his goal. True, a bank in a bush township was not a station in the bush itself. On the other hand, his would–be friend was not the first to warn Fergus against the futility of expecting more than a nominal salary as a babe and suckling in Colonial experience; and perhaps the prime elements of that experience might be gained as well in the purlieus of a sufficiently remote township as in realms unnamed on any map. It will be seen that the sober stripling was reduced to arguing with himself, and that his main argument was not to be admitted in his own heart. The mysterious eccentricity of his employer, coupled with the adventurous character of his alleged prospects, was what induced the lad to embrace both in defiance of an unimaginative hard–headedness which he aimed at rather than possessed.

With characteristic prudence he had left his baggage on board the river–steamer, and his own hands carried it piecemeal to the bank. This was a red–brick bungalow with an ample veranda, standing back from the future street that was as yet little better than a country road. The veranda commanded a long perspective of pines, but no further bricks and mortar, and but very few weather board walls. The yard behind the house was shut in by as many outbuildings as clustered about the small homesteads which Fergus had already beheld on the banks of the Murrumbidgee. The man in charge of the yard was palpably in liquor, a chronic condition from his general appearance, and Mr. Macbean discharged him on the spot with a decision which left no loophole for appeal. The woman in charge of the house adorned another plane of civilization; she was very deaf, and very outspoken on her introduction to the young gentleman, whose face she was pleased to approve, with the implied reservation that all faces were liars; but she served up the mutton of the country hot and tender; and Fergus Carrick, leaning back after an excellent repast, marvelled for the twentieth time that he was not to pay for it.

"A teetotaler, are ye?" said Macbean, mixing a third glass of whiskey, with the skull–cap on the back of his head. "And so was I at your age; but you're my very man. There are some it sets talking. Wait till the old lady turns in, and then you shall see what you shall see."

Fergus waited in increasing excitement. The day's events were worthier of a dream. To have set foot in Glenranald without knowing a soul in the place, and to find one's self comfortably housed at a good salary before night! There were moments when he questioned the complete sanity of his eccentric benefactor, who drank whiskey like water, both as to quantity and effect and who chuckled continuously in his huge gray beard. But such doubts only added to the excitement of the evening, which reached a climax when a lighted candle was thrust in at the door and the pair advised not to make a night of it by

4

the candid crone on her way to bed.

"We will give her twenty minutes," said the manager, winking across his glass. "I've never let her hear me, and she mustn't hear you either. She must know nothing at all about it; nobody must, except you and me."

The mystification of Fergus was now complete. Unimaginative as he was by practice and profession, he had an explanation a minute until the time was up, when the truth beat them all for wild improbability. Macbean had risen, lifting the lamp; holding it on high he led the way through baize doors into the banking premises. Here was another door, which Macbean not only unlocked, but locked again behind them both. A small inner office led them into a shuttered chamber of fair size, with a broad polished counter, glass swing–doors, and a formidable portal beyond. And one of young Carrick's theories received apparent confirmation on the spot; for the manager slipped behind his counter by another door, and at once whipped out a great revolver.

"This they provide us with," said he. "So far it is our only authorized defence, and it hangs on a hook down here behind the counter. But you march in here prepared, your pistol cocked behind your back, and which of us is likely to shoot first?"

"The bushranger," said Fergus, still rather more startled than reassured.

"The bushranger, of course. Stingaree, let us say. As for me, either my arms go up, or down I go in a heap. But supposing my arms do go up — supposing I still touch something with one foot — and supposing the floor just opens and swallows Mr. Sanguinary Stingaree! Eh? eh? What then?"

"It would be great," cried Fergus. "But could it be done?"

"It can be, it will be, and is being done," replied the manager, replacing the bank revolver and sliding over the counter like a boy. A square of plain linoleum covered the floor, overlapped by a border of the same material bearing a design. Down went Macbean upon his knees, and his beard swept this border as he began pulling it up, tacks and all.

The lamp burned brightly on the counter, its rays reflected in the burnished mahogany. All at once Fergus seized it on his own initiative, and set it on the floor before his

5

kneeling elder, going upon his own knees on the other side. And where the plain linoleum ended, but where the overlapping border covered the floor, the planks were sawn through and through down one side of the central and self–colored square.

"A trap–door!" exclaimed Fergus in a whisper.

Macbean leant back on his slippered heels, his skull–cap wickedly awry.

"This border takes a lot o' lifting," said he. "Yet we've just got to lift it every time, and tack it down again before morning. You might try your hand over yonder on the far side."

Fergus complied with so much energy that the whole border was ripped up in a minute; and he was not mistaken. A trap–door it was, of huge dimensions, almost exactly covered by the self–colored square; but at each side a tongue of linoleum had been left loose for lifting it; and the lamp had scarcely been replaced upon the counter when the bulk of the floor leaned upright in one piece against the opposite wall. It had uncovered a pit of corresponding size, but as yet hardly deep enough to afford a hiding–place for the bucket, spade, and pickaxe which lay there on a length of sacking.

"I see!" exclaimed Carrick, as the full light flooded his brain.

"Is that a fact?" inquired the manager twinkling.

"You're going to make a deep hole of it ——?"

"No. I'm going to pay you to make it deep for me ——"

"And then ——"

"At dead o' night; you can take out your sleep by day."

"When Stingaree comes ——"

"If he waits till we're ready for him ——"

"You touch some lever ——"

6

The Black Hole of Glenranald

"And the floor swallows him, as I said, if he waits till we are ready for him. Everything depends on that — and on your silence. We must take time. It isn't only the digging of the hole. We need to fix up some counterpoise to make it shut after a body like a mouse–trap; we must do the thing thoroughly if we do it at all; and till it's done, not a word to a soul in the same hemisphere! In the end I suppose I shall have to tell Donkin, my cashier, and Fowler the clerk. Donkin's a disbeliever who deserves the name o' Didymus more than ony mon o' my acquaintance. Fowler would take so kindly to the whole idea that he'd blurt it out within a week. He may find it out when all's in readiness, but I'll no tell him even then. See how I trust a brither Scot at sight!"

"I much appreciate it," said Fergus, humbly.

"I wouldna ha' trustit even you, gin I hadna found the delvin' ill worrk for auld shoulders," pursued Macbean, broadening his speech with intentional humor. "Noo, wull ye do't or wull ye no?"

The young man's answer was to strip off his coat and spring into the hole, and to set to work with such energy, yet so quietly, that the bucket was filled in a few almost silent seconds. Macbean carried it off, unlocking doors for the nonce, while Fergus remained in the hole to mop his forehead.

"We need to have another bucket," said the manager, on his return. "I've thought of every other thing. There's a disused well in the yard, and down goes every blessed bucket!"

To and fro, over the lip of the closing well, back into the throat of the deepening hole, went the buckets for many a night; and by day Fergus Carrick employed his best wits to make an intrinsically anomalous position appear natural to the world. It was a position which he himself could thoroughly enjoy; he was largely his own master. He had daily opportunities of picking up the ways and customs of the bush, and a nightly excitement which did not pall as the secret task approached conclusion; but he was subjected to much chaff and questioning from the other young bloods of Glenranald. He felt from the first that it was what he must expect. He was a groom with a place at his master's table; he was a jackeroo who introduced station life into a town. And the element of underlying mystery, really existing as it did, was detected soon enough by other young heads, led by that of Fowler, the keen bank clerk.

"I was looking at you both together, and you do favor the old man, and no error!" he would say; or else, "What is it you could hang the boss for, Fergy, old toucher?"

These delicate but cryptic sallies being ignored or parried, the heavy swamp of innuendo was invariably deserted for the breezy hill–top of plain speech, and Fergus had often work enough to put a guard upon hand and tongue. But his temperament was eminently self–contained, and on the whole he was an elusive target for the witticisms of his friends. There was no wit, however, and no attempt at it on the part of Donkin, the cantankerous cashier. He seldom addressed a word to Carrick, never a civil word, but more than once he treated his chief to a sarcastic remonstrance on his degrading familiarity with an underling. In such encounters the imperturbable graybeard was well able to take care of himself, albeit he expressed to Fergus a regret that he had not exercised a little more ingenuity in the beginning.

"You should have come to me with a letter of introduction," said he.

"But who would have given me one?"

"I would, yon first night, and you'd have presented it next day in office hours," replied the manager. "But it's too late to think about it now, and in a few days Donkin may know the truth."

He might have known it already, but for one difficulty. They had digged their pit to the generous depth of eight feet, so that a tall prisoner could barely touch the trap–door with extended fingertips; and Stingaree (whose latest performance was no longer the Yallarook affair) was of medium height according to his police description. The trap–door was a double one, which parted in the centre with the deadly precision of the gallows floor. The difficulty was to make the flaps close automatically, with the mouse–trap effect of Macbean's ambition. It was managed eventually by boring separate wells for a weight behind the hinges on either side. Copper wire running on minute pulleys let into grooves suspended these weights and connected them with the flaps, and powerful door–springs supplemented the more elaborate contrivance. The lever controlling the whole was concealed under the counter, and reached by thrusting a foot through a panel, which also opened inward on a spring.

The Black Hole of Glenranald

It may be conceived that all this represented the midnight labors and the constant thought of many weeks. It was now the beginning of the cool but brilliant Riverina winter, and, despite the disparity in their years, the two Scotsmen were fast friends. They had worked together as one man, with the same patient passion for perfection, the same delight in detail for its own sake. Almost the only difference was that the old fellow refreshed his energies with the glass of whiskey which was never far from his elbow after banking hours, while the young one cultivated the local excess of continual tea. And all this time the rascally Stingaree ranged the district, with or without his taciturn accomplice, covering great distances in fabulous time, lurking none knew where, and springing on the unwary in the last places in which his presence was suspected.

"But he has not yet robbed a bank, and we have our hopes," wrote Fergus to a faithful sister at Largs. "It may be for fear of the revolvers with which all the banks are provided now. Mr. Macbean has been practising with ours, and purposely put a bullet through one of our back windows. The whole township has been chafing him about it, and the local rag has risen to a sarcastic paragraph, which is exactly what we wanted. The trap–door over the pit is now practically finished. It's too complicated to describe, but Stingaree has only to march into the bank and 'stick it up' and the man behind the counter has only to touch a lever with his foot for the villain to disappear through the floor into a prison it'll take him all his time to break. On Saturday the cashier and the clerk are coming to dinner, and before we sit down they are to be shown everything."

This was but a fraction of one of the long letters which Fergus despatched by nearly every mail. Silent and self–contained as he was, he had one confidante at the opposite end of the earth, one escape–pipe in his pen. Not a word of the great secret had he even written to another soul. To his trusted sister he had never before been quite so communicative. His conscience pricked him as he took his letter to the post, and he had it registered on no other score.

On Saturday the bank closed at one o'clock; the staff were to return and dine at seven, the Queen's birthday falling on the same day for a sufficient pretext. As the hour approached Fergus made the distressing discovery that his friend and host had anticipated the festivities with too free a hand. Macbean was not drunk, but he was perceptibly blunted and blurred, and Fergus had never seen the pale eyes so watery or the black skull–cap so much on one side of the venerable head. The lad was genuinely grieved. A whiskey bottle stood empty on the laden board, and he had the temerity to pocket the corkscrew while

The Black Hole of Glenranald

Macbean was gone to his storeroom for another bottle. A solemn search ensued, and then Fergus was despatched in haste for a new corkscrew.

"An' look slippy," said Macbean, "or we'll have old Donkin here before ye get back."

"Not for another three–quarters of an hour," remarked Fergus, looking at his watch.

"Any minute!" retorted Macbean, with a ribald epithet. "I invited Donkin, in confidence, to come a good half–hour airly, and I'll tell ye for why. Donkin must ken, but I'm none so sure o' yon other impident young squirt. His tongue's too long for his mouth. Donkin or I could always be behind the counter; anyway, I mean to take his opeenion before tellin' any other body."

Entertaining his own distrust of the vivacious Fowler, Fergus commended the decision, and so took his departure by the private entrance. It was near sundown; a fresh breeze blew along the hard road, puffing cloudlets of yellow sand into the rosy dusk. Fergus hurried till he was out of sight, and then idled shamelessly under trees. He was not going on for a new corkscrew. He was going back to confess boldly where he had found the old one. And the sight of Donkin in the distance sent him back in something of a hurry; it was quite enough to have to spend an evening with the cantankerous cashier.

The bank was practically at one end of the township as then laid out; two or three buildings there were further on, but they stood altogether aloof. The bank, for a bank, was sufficiently isolated, and Fergus could not but congratulate himself on the completion of its ingenious and unsuspected defences. It only remained to keep the inventor reasonably sober for the evening, and thereafter to whistle or to pray for Stingaree. Meanwhile the present was no mean occasion, and Fergus was glad to see that Macbean had thrown open the official doors in his absence. They had often agreed that it would be worth all their labor to enlighten Donkin by letting the pit gape under his nose as he entered the bank. Fergus glanced over his shoulder, saw the other hurrying, and hurried himself in order to take up a good position for seeing the cashier's face. He was in the middle of the treacherous floor before he perceived that it was not Macbean in the half–light behind the counter, but a good–looking man whom he had never seen before.

"Didn't know I was invited, eh?" said the stranger, putting up a single eye–glass. "Don't believe it, perhaps? You'd better ask Mr. Macbean!"

The Black Hole of Glenranald

And before it had occurred to him to stir from where he stood agape, the floor fell from under the feet of Fergus, his body lurched forward, and came down flat and heavy on the hard earth eight feet below. Not entirely stunned, though shaken and hurt from head to heel, he was still collecting his senses when the pit blackened as the trap–door shut in implicit obedience to its weights and springs. And in the clinging velvet darkness the young man heard a groan.

"Is that yoursel', Fergy?"

"And are you there, Mr. Macbean?"

"Mon, didn't it shut just fine!"

Curiously blended with the physical pain in the manager's voice was a sodden philosophic humor which maddened the younger man. Fergus swore where he lay writhing on his stomach. Macbean chuckled and groaned again.

"It's Stingaree," he said, drawing a breath through his teeth.

"Of course it is."

"I never breathed it to a soul."

"No more did I."

Fergus spoke with ready confidence, and yet the words left something on his mind. It was something vague but haunting, something that made him feel instinctively unworthy of the kindly, uncomplaining tone which had annoyed him but a moment before.

"No bones broken, Fergy?"

"None that I know of."

"I doubt I've not been so lucky. I'm thinkin' it's a rib, by the way it hurts to breathe."

The Black Hole of Glenranald

Fergus was already fumbling in his pocket. The match–box opened with a click. The match scraped several times in vain. Then at last the scene sprang out as on the screen of a magic–lantern. And to Fergus it was a very white old man, hunched up against the muddy wall, with blood upon his naked scalp and beard, and both hands pressed to his side; to the old man, a muddy face stricken with horrified concern, and a match burning down between muddy fingers; but to both, such a new view and version of their precious hole that the corners of each mouth were twitching as the match was thrown away.

Fergus was fumbling for another when a step rang overhead; and at the sharp exchange of words which both underground expected, Fergus came on all fours to the old man's side, and together they sat gazing upward into the pall of impenetrable crape.

"You infernal villain!" they heard Donkin roar, and stamp his feet with such effect that the floor opened, and down through the square of light came the cashier feet first.

"Heaven and hell!" he squealed, but subsided unhurt on hands and knees as the flaps went up with such a snap that Macbean and Carrick nudged each other at the same moment. "Now I know who you are!" the cashier raved. "Call yourself Stingaree! You're Fowler dressed up, and this is one of Macbean's putrid practical jokes. I saw his jackal hurrying in to say I was coming. By cripes! it takes a surgical operation to see their sort, I grant you."

There was a noise of subdued laughter overhead; even in the pit a dry chuckle came through Macbean's set teeth.

"If it's practical joke o' mine, Donkin, it's recoiled on my own poor pate," said the old man. "I've a rib stove in, too, if that's any consolation to ye. It's Stingaree, my manny!"

"You're right, it is, it must be!" cried the cashier, finding his words in a torrent. "I was going to tell you. He's been at his game down south; stuck up our own mail again only yesterday, between this and Deniliquin, and got a fine haul of registered letters, so they say. But where the deuce are we? I never knew there was a cellar under here, let alone a trap–door that might have been made for these villains."

"It was made for them," replied Macbean, after a pause; and in the dead dark he went on to relate the frank and humble history of the hole, from its inception to the crooked

12

climax of that bitter hour. A braver confession Fergus had never heard; its philosophic flow was unruffled by the more and more scornful interjections of the ungenerous cashier; and yet his younger countryman, who might have been proud of him, hardly listened to a word uttered by Macbean.

Half–a–dozen fallen from the lips of Donkin had lightened young Carrick's darkness with consuming fires of shame. "A fine haul of registered letters" — among others his own last letter to his sister! So it was he who had done it all; and he had perjured himself to his benefactor, besides, betraying him. He sat in the dark between fire and ice, chiefly wondering how he could soonest win through the trap–door and earn a bullet in his brain.

"The spree to–night," concluded Macbean, whose fall completely sobered him, "was for the express purpose of expounding the trap to you, and I asked you airly to take your advice. I was no so sure about young Fowler, whether we need tell him or no. He has an awful long tongue; but I'm thinkin' there's a longer if I knew where to look for it."

"I could tell you where," rasped Donkin. "But go on."

"I was watching old Hannah putting her feenishing touches to the table, and waiting for Fergus Carrick to come back, when I thought I heard him behind me and you with him. But it was Stingaree and his mate, and the two of us were covered with revolvers like young rifles. Hannah they told to go on with what she was doing, as they were mighty hungry, and I advised her to do as she was bid. The brute with the beard has charge of her. Stingaree himself drove me into the middle of my own trap–door, made me give up my keys, and then went behind the counter and did the trick. He'd got it all down on paper, the Lord alone knows how."

"Oh, you Scotchmen!" cried the pleasant cashier. "Talk of your land of cakes! You take every cake in the land between you!"

It seemed he had been filling his pipe while he listened and prepared this pretty speech. Now he struck a match, and with the flame to the bowl saw Fergus for the first time. The cashier held the match on high.

"You here all the while?" he cried. "No wonder you lay low, Carrick; no wonder I didn't hear your voice."

The Black Hole of Glenranald

"What do you mean by that?" growled Fergus, in fierce heat and fierce satisfaction.

"Surely, Mr. Macbean, you aren't wondering who wagged the long tongue now?"

"You mean that I wagged mine? And it's a lie!" said Fergus, hoarsely; he was sitting upon his heels, poised to spring.

"I mean that if Mr. Macbean had listened to me two months ago we should none of us be in this hole now."

"Then, my faith, you're in a worse one than you think!" cried Fergus, and fell upon his traducer as the match went out. "Take that, and that, and that!" he ground out through his teeth, as he sent the cashier over on his back and pounded the earth with his skull. Luckily the first was soft and the second hard, so that the man was more outraged than hurt when circumstances which they might have followed created a diversion.

In his turn the lively Fowler had marched whistling into the bank, had ceased whistling to swear down the barrel of a cocked revolver, and met a quicker fate than his comrades by impressing the bushranger as the most dangerous man of the quartette. Unfortunately for him, his fate was still further differentiated from theirs. Fowler's feet glanced off Carrick's back, and he plunged into the well head–first, rolling over like a stone as the wooden jaws above closed greedily upon the light of day.

Fergus at once struck matches, and in their light the cashier took the insensible head upon his knees and glared at his enemy as if from sanctuary of the Red Cross. But Fergus returned to Macbean's side.

"I never said a word to a living soul," he muttered. "It has come out some other way."

"Of course it has," said the old manager, with the same tell–tale inhalation through the teeth. Fergus felt worse than ever. He groped for the bald head and found it cold and dank. In an instant he was clamoring under the trap–door, leaping up and striking it with his fist.

"What do you want?"

The Black Hole of Glenranald

"Whiskey. Some of us are hurt."

"God help you if it's any hanky–panky!"

"It's none. Something to drink, and something to drink it in, or there's blood upon your head!"

Clanking steps departed and returned.

"Stand by to catch, below there!"

And Fergus stood by, expecting to see a long barrel with the bottle and glass that broke their fall on him; but Stingaree had crept away unheard, and he pressed the lever just enough to let the glass and bottle tumble through.

Time passed: it might have been an hour. The huddled heap that was Macbean breathed forth relief. The head on Donkin's knees moved from side to side with groans. Donkin himself thanked Fergus for his ration; he who served it out alone went thirsty. "Wait till I earn some," he said bitterly to himself. "I could finish the lot if I started now." But the others never dreamt that he was waiting, and he lied about it to Macbean.

Now that they sat in silence no sound escaped them overhead. They heard Stingaree and his mate sit down to a feast which Macbean described with groaning modesty as the best that he could do.

"There's no soup," he whispered, "but there's a barr'l of oysters fetched up on purpose by the coach. I hope they havena missed the Chablis. They may as well do the thing complete." In a little the champagne popped. "Dry Monopole!" moaned the manager, near to tears. "It came up along with the oysters. O sirs, O sirs, but this is hard on us all! Now they're at the turkey — and I chopped the stuffing with my ain twa han's!"

They were at the turkey a long time. Another cork popped; but the familiar tread of deaf Hannah was heard no more, and at length they called her.

"Mother!" roared a mouth that was full.

The Black Hole of Glenranald

"Old lady!" cried the gallant Stingaree.

"She's 'ard of 'earing, mate."

"She might still hear you, Howie."

And the chairs rasped backward over bare boards as one; at the same instant Fergus leapt to his feet in the earthly Tartarus his own hands had dug.

"I do believe she's done a bolt," he gasped, "and got clean away!"

Curses overhead confirmed the supposition. Clanking feet hunted the premises at a run. In a minute the curses were renewed and multiplied, yet muffled, as though there was some fresh cause for them which the prisoners need not know. Hannah had not been found. Yet some disturbing discovery had undoubtedly been made. Doors were banged and bolted. A gunshot came faint but staccato from the outer world. A real report echoed through the bank.

"A siege!" cried Fergus, striking a match to dance by. "The old heroine has fetched the police, and these beauties are in a trap."

"And what about us?" demanded the cashier.

"Shut up and listen!" retorted Fergus, without ceremony. Macbean was leaning forward, with bald head on one side and hollowed palm at the upper ear. Even the stunned man had recovered sufficiently to raise himself on one elbow and gaze overhead as Fergus struck match after match. The villains were having an altercation on the very trap–door.

"Now's the time to cut and run — now or never."

"Very well, you do so. I'm going through the safe."

"You should ha' done that first."

"Better late than not at all."

The Black Hole of Glenranald

"You can't stop and do it without me."

"Oh, yes, I can. I'll call for a volunteer from below. You show them your spurs and save your skin."

"Oh, I'll stay, curse you, I'll stay!"

"And I'll have my volunteer, whether you stay or not."

The pair had scarcely parted when the trap-door opened slowly and stayed open for the first time. The banking chamber was but dimly lit, and the light in the pit less than it had been during the brief burning of single matches. No peering face was revealed to those below, but the voice of Stingaree came rich and crisp from behind the counter.

"Your old woman has got away to the police-barracks and the place is surrounded. One of you has got to come up and help, and help fair, or go to hell with a bullet in his heart. I give you one minute to choose your man."

But in one second the man had chosen himself. Without a word, or a glance at any of his companions, but with a face burning with extraordinary fires, Fergus Carrick sprang for the clean edge of the trap-door, caught it first with one hand and then with both, drew himself up like the gymnast he had been at his Scottish school, and found himself prone upon the floor and trap-door as the latter closed under him on the release of the lever which Stingaree understood so well. A yell of execration followed him into the upper air. And Stingaree was across the counter before his new ally had picked himself up.

"That's because this was expected of me," said Fergus, grimly, to explain the cashier's reiterated anathemas. "I was the writer of the registered letter that led to all this. So now I'm going the whole hog."

And the blue eyes boiled in his brick-red face.

"You mean that? No nonsense?"

"You shall see."

The Black Hole of Glenranald

"I should shoot you like a native cat."

"You couldn't do me a better turn."

"Right! Swear on your knees that you won't use it against me or my mate, and I'll trust you with this revolver. You may fire as high as you please, but they must think we're three instead of two."

Fergus took the oath in fierce earnest upon his knees, was handed the weapon belonging to the bank, and posted in his own bedroom window at the rear of the building. The front was secure enough with the shutters and bolts of the official fortress. It was to the back premises that the attack confined itself, making all use of the admirable cover afforded by the stables.

Carrick saw heads and shoulders hunched to aim over stable–doors as he obeyed his orders and kept his oath. His high fire drew a deadlier upon himself; a stream of lead from a Winchester whistled into the room past his ear and over his ducked head. He tried firing from the floor without showing his face. The Winchester let him alone; in a sudden sickness he sprang up to see if anything hung sprawling over the stable–door, and was in time to see men in retreat to right and left, the white pugarees of the police fluttering ingloriously among them. Only one was left upon the ground, and he could sit up to nurse a knee.

Fergus sighed relief as he sought Stingaree, and found him with a comical face before the open safe.

"House full of paltry paper!" said he. "I suppose it's the old sportsman's custom to get rid of most of his heavy metal before closing on Saturdays?"

Fergus said it was; he had himself stowed many a strong–box aboard unsuspected barges for Echuca.

"Well, now's our time to leave you," continued Stingaree. "If I'm not mistaken, their flight is simply for the moment, and in two or three more they'll be back to batter in the bank shutters. I wonder what they think we've done with our horses? I'll bet they've looked everywhere but in the larder next the kitchen door — not that we ever let them get so close. But my mate's in there now, mounted and waiting, and I shall have to leave you."

"But I was coming with you," cried Fergus, aghast.

Stingaree's eye–glass dangled on its cord.

"I'm afraid I must trouble you to step into that safe instead," said he, smiling.

"Man, I mean it! You think I don't. I've fought on your side of my own free will. How can I live that down? It's the only side for me for the rest of time!"

The fixed eye–glass covered the brick–red face with the molten eyes.

"I believe you do mean it."

"You shall shoot me if I don't."

"I most certainly should. But my mate Howie has his obvious limitations. I've long wanted a drop of new blood. Barmaid's thoroughbred and strong as an elephant; we're neither of us heavyweights; by the powers, I'll trust you, and you shall ride behind!"

Now, Barmaid was the milk–white mare that was only less notorious than her lawless rider. It was noised in travellers' huts and around campfires that she would do more at her master's word than had been known of horse outside a circus. It was the one touch that Stingaree had borrowed from a more Napoleonic but incomparably coarser and crueller knight of the bush. In all other respects the fin de siècle desperado was unique. It was a stroke of luck, however, that there happened to be an old white mare in the bank stables, which the police had impounded with solemn care while turning every other animal adrift. And so it fell out that not a shot followed the mounted bushrangers into the night, and that long before the bank shutters were battered in the flying trio were miles away.

Fergus flew like a runaway bride, his arms about the belted waist of Stingaree. Trees loomed ahead and flew past by the clump under a wonderful wide sky of scintillating stars. The broad bush track had very soon been deserted at a tangent; through ridges and billows of salt–bush and cotton–bush they sailed with the swift confidence of a well–handled clipper before the wind. Stingaree was the leader four miles out of five, but in the fifth his mate Howie would gallop ahead, and anon they would come on him dismounted at a wire fence, with the wires strapped down and his horse tethered to one of the posts till he had led Barmaid over.

It was thus they careered across the vast chessboard of the fenced back–blocks at dead of night. Stingaree and Fergus sat saddle and bareback without a break until near dawn their pioneer spurred forward yet again and was swallowed in a steely haze. It was cold as a sharp spring night in England. But for a mile or more Fergus had clung on with but one arm round the bushranger's waist; now the right arm came stealing back; felt something cold for the fraction of a second, and plucked prodigiously, and in another fraction an icy ring mouthed Stingaree's neck.

"Pull up," said Fergus, hoarsely, "or your brains go flying."

"Little traitor!" whispered the other, with an imprecation that froze the blood.

"I am no traitor. I swore I wouldn't abuse the revolver you gave me, and it's been in my pocket all the night."

"The other's unloaded."

"You wouldn't sit so quiet if it were. Now, round we go, and back on our tracks full split. It's getting light, and we shall see them plain. If you vary a yard either way, or if your mate catches us, out go your brains."

The bushranger obeyed without a word. Fergus was almost unnerved by the incredible ease of his conquest over so redoubtable a ruffian. His stolid Scottish blood stood by him; but still he made grim apology as they rode.

"I had to do it. It was through me you got to know. I had to live that down; this was the only way."

"You have spirit. If you would still be my mate ——"

20

The Black Hole of Glenranald

"Your mate! I mean this to be the making of me as an honest man. Here's the fence. I give you two minutes to strap it down and get us over."

Stingaree slid tamely to the ground.

"Don't you dare to get through those wires! Strap it from this side with your belt, and strap it quick!"

And the bushranger obeyed with the same sensible docility, but with his back turned, so that Fergus could not see has face; and it was light enough to see faces now; yet Barmaid refused the visible wires, as she had not refused them all that night of indigo starlight.

"Coax her, man!" cried Fergus, in the saddle now, and urging the mare with his heels. So Stingaree whispered in the mare's ear; and with that the strapped wires flew under his captor's nose, as the rider took the fence, but not the horse.

At a single syllable the milk—white mare had gone on her knees, like devout lady in holy fane; and as she rose her last rider lay senseless at her master's feet; but whether from his fall, or from a blow dealt him in the act of falling, the unhappy Fergus never knew. Indeed, knowledge for him was at an end until matches burnt under his nose awakened him to a position of the last humiliation. His throat and chin topped a fence—post, the weight of his body was on chin and throat, while wrists and muscles were lashed at full stretch to the wires on either side.

"Now I'm going to shoot you like a dog," said Stingaree. He drew the revolver whose muzzle had pressed into his own neck so short a time before. Yet now it was broad daylight, and the sun coming up in the bound youth's eyes for the last time.

"Shoot away!" he croaked, raising the top of his head to speak at all. "I gave you leave before we started. Shoot away!"

"At ten paces," said Stingaree, stepping them. "That, I think, is fair."

"Perfectly," replied Fergus. "But be kind enough to make this so—called man of yours hold his foul tongue till I'm out of earshot of you all."

The Black Hole of Glenranald

Huge Howie had muttered little enough for him, but to that little Stingaree put an instantaneous stop.

"He's a dog, to be shot like a dog, but too good a dog for you to blackguard!" cried he. "Any message, young fellow?"

"Not through you."

"So long, then!"

"Shoot away!"

The long barrel was poised as steadily as field– gun on its carriage. Fergus kept his blue eyes on the gleaming ring of the muzzle.

The hammer fell, the cartridge cracked, and from the lifted muzzle a tiny cloud flowed like a bubble from a pipe. The post quivered under Carrick's chin, and a splinter flew up and down before his eyes. But that was all.

"Aim longer," said he. "Get it over this shot."

"I'll try."

But the same thing happened again.

"Come nearer," sneered Fergus.

And Stingaree strode forward with an oath.

"I was going to give you six of them. But you're a braver man than I thought. And that's the lot."

The bound youth's livid face turned redder than the red dawn.

"Shoot me — shoot!" he shouted, like a lunatic.

The Black Hole of Glenranald

"No, I shall not. I never meant to — I did mean you to sit out six — but you're the most gallant little idiot I've ever struck. Besides, you come from the old country, like myself!"

And a sigh floated into the keen morning air as he looked his last upon the lad through the celebrated monocle.

"Then I'll shoot myself when I'm free," sobbed Fergus through his teeth.

"Oh, no, you won't," were Stingaree's last words. "You'll find it's not a bit worth while."

And when the mounted police and others from Glenranald discovered the trussed youngster, not an hour later, they took the same tone. And one and all stopped and stooped to peer at the two bullet–holes in the post, and at something underneath them, before cutting poor Fergus down.

Then they propped him up to read with his own eyes the nailed legend which first helped Fergus Carrick to live down the indiscretion of his letter to Largs, and then did more for him in that Colony than letter from Queen Victoria to His Excellency of New South Wales. For it ran:—

"THIS IS THE GAMEST LITTLE COCK I HAVE EVER STRUCK. HE HAD ME CAPTIVE ONCE, COULD HAVE SHOT ME OVER AND OVER AGAIN, AND ALL BUT TOOK ME ALIVE. MORE POWER TO HIM!

"STINGAREE."

LaVergne, TN USA
15 November 2010
204989LV00005B/111/A

9 781419 154188